A MESSAGE FROM CHICKEN HOUSE

Sometimes stories start just *right*. Occasionally they get even better. Hardly ever does the same story end super-satisfyingly. Heather Dyer manages all three!

BARRY CUNNINGHAM
Publisher
Chicken House

Text © Heather Dyer 2005
Illustrations © Peter Bailey 2005

First published in Great Britain in 2005
This edition published in 2018
Chicken House
2 Palmer Street
Frome, Somerset BA11 1DS
United Kingdom
www.chickenhousebooks.com

Cover design by Helen Crawford-White
Cover illustration by Mellisa Castrillón
Designed and typeset by Ian Butterworth
Interior illustrations by Peter Bailey
Printed and bound in Great Britain by CPI Group (UK) Ltd, Croydon CR0 4YY

1 3 5 7 9 10 8 6 4 2

British Library Cataloguing in Publication data available.

PB ISBN 978-1-911490-24-1

THE GIRL WITH THE BROKEN WING

HEATHER DYER

Chicken House

2 Palmer Street, Frome, Somerset BA11 1DS
www.chickenhousebooks.com

1
The Crash Landing

Chimneys can be dangerous. Imagine it: a dark night and you're flying low over the rooftops, barely skimming the tiles. The wind is gusting and buffeting you off-course and the rain is getting in your eyes so you can hardly see where you're going. And then, just as you're coming in to land there's a sudden gust of wind and – WHAM!

The twins were in bed when it happened. They heard a sound like a wet cabbage hitting a wall, then a clattering on the tiles – then nothing but the wind wuthering round the eaves once more.

'What was that?' whispered James.

Amanda, who slept behind a curtain on the other side of the attic, switched on her bedside light and they lay very still, listening.

Rap-rap! came a knock on the skylight.

'Who's there?' said James. He climbed out of bed and stood under the window, and there he saw a startled face framed by a tangle of windblown hair. 'It's a girl!' he cried.

Together, the twins dragged across the big red chair from the corner, and James stood on it to reach the catch.

'Open up!' yelled the girl in a muffled voice.

James opened the window and a gust of rain blew into the room. 'Thanks,' gasped the girl, climbing through – and a moment later she was standing there before them, dripping on the carpet. To the twins' astonishment they saw that she was barefoot and wearing only a thin, white cotton dress. But most astonishing of all, hanging from her shoulders and reaching nearly to her feet, was a pair of long white wings.

'Ow,' moaned the girl, clutching her left shoulder. 'I think I've broken my wing.'

James and Amanda helped the girl with the broken wing to the sofa, where she sat down carefully. 'I'll have to lie on my front,' she said.

So Amanda brought a pillow and the girl lay down with her long white wings folded neatly along her back. The tips of the wings lay on her calves and the downy feathers at her shoulders were sticky with rain. Amanda put out a hand and stroked one of the wings gently. It felt firm and springy, like stroking a swan.

'What's your name?' asked Amanda.

The girl with the broken wing yawned. 'Hilary,' she said.

'I'm Amanda,' said Amanda politely. 'And this is my brother, James.'

'Nice to meet you,' murmured Hilary, snuggling deeper into the pillow.

'Um – Hilary,' said James. 'What were you doing on our roof?'

Hilary mumbled something that neither

of them could quite make out, then closed her eyes.

'Pardon?' said James.

But there was no reply. Hilary's breathing had settled into the regular, easy rhythm of sleep.

'She's had a shock,' said Amanda. 'We'll ask her again in the morning.'

Then, just as they were about to turn away, Hilary opened her eyes and spoke again – quite clearly this time.

'Good night!' she said.

2
The Angel Question

The first thing the twins remembered when the alarm went off was the girl with the broken wing – and there she was, still sleeping soundly on the sofa. They crept out of bed and stood looking down at her. She slept with one arm flopped over the side, and the wings on her back rose and fell gently with her breathing.

'Do you think she's an angel?' whispered Amanda.

James shook his head. 'Angels don't snore,' he said.

They watched her sleeping. Her elbow was grazed – probably from her crash landing the night before – and the soles of her feet were filthy.

'Perhaps we should wake her up,' said Amanda.

James hesitated. Then he leant down and said softly, '*Hilary!*' But Hilary slept on, undisturbed. He tried again, a little louder this time. '*Hilary!*'

Still nothing.

'*HILARY!*' he shouted.

Hilary's eyelids twitched, but did not open.

'It's eight o'clock,' said James, looking at his watch. 'We've got to go.'

'We can't just leave her.'

The twins considered. Amanda thought that they ought to tell their parents about Hilary, but James didn't think they should. 'I don't think they believe in girls with broken wings,' he said. 'They might call the police, or something.'

This was true.

'Well, we can't throw her out,' said Amanda. 'Not with a broken wing. We'll have to hide her in our room and bring her food until she's well enough to fly again.'

They looked at Hilary. She looked as though she could go on sleeping all day long.

'But what if she wakes up and goes downstairs?' said James. 'Or what if Mum comes up and sees her?'

'We'll write her a note,' said Amanda, and she ran to get her sketchpad and a green pencil, while James thought of what to say.

'Tell her we'll be back at four o'clock,' said James.

There was a long pause while Amanda scribbled it down.

'And tell her not to go downstairs.'

Amanda scribbled that down, too.

'And say that if she hears anyone coming up the stairs she has to hide in the wardrobe.'

'Right,' said Amanda. When she had finished writing she folded the note and wrote 'HILARY' on the front, with a smiley face. Then she put her sketchpad, some coloured pencils and a bag of chocolate buttons beside the sofa, and balanced the note on top. Then they hurried down the stairs.

It's hard to believe that you've got a girl with a broken wing in your bedroom when you're bumping along in a school bus with people yelling all around you and throwing crisps across the aisle. James and Amanda took a seat near the front of the bus to discuss her.

'Where do you think she's come from?' asked James.

'Heaven,' said Amanda simply. 'That's

where *all* the angels come from.'

James grunted. 'She doesn't look much like an angel to me.'

'How do you know? You've never seen one.'

'I've read about them,' said James. 'They wear long robes and their heads are all lit up like light bulbs.'

'That's not their heads, that's their halos.'

'And anyway,' said James, 'there aren't *really* any angels. If there were, you'd see them on the news.'

James was a neat, logical person who parted his hair on the side and kept his things in boxes with lids on. If there had ever been an angel in the news, he would know. Amanda, on the other hand, was the sort of girl who wore her long red hair in pigtails and sewed flower patches onto the back pockets of her jeans. Also, she read a lot of fiction, so she knew that *anything* was possible.

'And if she *was* an angel,' said James, 'what would she be doing on our roof?'

'Maybe she's a guardian angel,' said Amanda. 'They're the ones that get sent to Earth to help people.'

James snorted.

'It's true!' said Amanda.

'All right, then,' said James. 'When we get home we'll ask her straight out and see what she says.'

'We can't do that!' said Amanda indignantly. 'Anyway – I *know* she's an angel. You're the one who isn't sure – *you* ask her.'

'*I'm* not asking,' said James. 'Because I know she isn't. There's no such thing.'

'There might be.'

'There isn't. Ask anyone – ask a scientist!'

'All right,' said Amanda. 'We'll ask Mr Lock at lunchtime. He'll know.'

Mr Lock was the teacher who knew most

about science. Whenever there was going to be something happening in the sky, like a comet or an eclipse, he always told his class so that they could go outside at night and look at it. And he made his own wine, too, at home. Mr Lock spent his lunch hour in the back of his classroom, perched on a stool among heaps of broken Bunsen burners and empty brown jars. He put away his sandwich hastily when the twins came in.

'What can I do for you?' he asked.

'We were wondering about angels,' said Amanda.

'Angels?' said Mr Lock. 'Is there a question about angels in the curriculum?'

'No,' said James. 'There isn't. We just wanted to know – could there be one?'

'A question?'

'No, an angel.'

'Well now,' said Mr Lock, brushing crumbs from his white coat. 'We'll need the board for this one.'

James and Amanda exchanged a weary look, but followed Mr Lock into the empty classroom.

'Are angels real ..?' said Mr Lock, wiping off a lot of calculations on the board. 'Ah yes ... once upon a time that was the question *everyone* wanted the answer to, and a very clever man called Leonardo Da Vinci looked into it. See here—' He took up a stub of chalk and began sketching.

'Leonardo's theory was that in order to fly, an angel's wings had to be this big.' He drew a man with enormous wings spread out behind him. 'And to get lift-off an angel's flight muscles would have had to have been supported by a breastbone *this* big.' He drew an enormous sticking-out chest on the angel, like on a cooked turkey. 'Of course, Leonardo deduced that it would have been impossible,' concluded Mr Lock, turning to the twins. 'An angel would have been *far too heavy to fly.*'

'Oh,' said Amanda, disappointed.

'What about a girl angel?' said James. 'A small one?'

'Apparently,' said Mr Lock, rubbing out the angel with the turkey chest, 'all the angels were men.'

So that solved it. Hilary couldn't be an angel after all – could she?

'Told you,' said James to Amanda.

Amanda was not convinced, but she said nothing.

3
Hilary in Trouble

The afternoon dragged on. The twins couldn't help but wonder what Hilary was doing at home, and whether she would still be there when they got back. Neither of them could concentrate on their lessons, and for the first time ever Amanda got told off for not paying attention. It seemed like forever before they found themselves back on the school bus and pulling into the stop at the end of their street.

'I hope she's all right,' said Amanda, as they stepped off the bus. 'I hope she wasn't bored.'

'Never mind,' said James. 'As soon as we get in we'll—' He stopped suddenly.

'Oh, *no!*' cried Amanda.

They could see Hilary from the bus stop. She was standing on the roof of their house in her thin white dress with her long white wings jutting out behind her – and she seemed to be throwing pointy white objects onto the lawn.

Without a word, the twins rushed home and ran straight up the stairs – not even stopping to let their mother take their coats. James jumped up on the red chair and put his head out through the skylight. 'Hilary!' he hissed.

Hilary started, and turned around. The front of her dress was smeared with chocolate, and there were paper aeroplanes littered all over the roof. '*Finally!*' she said. 'Where have you *been?*

I've been waiting for—'

'Get inside!' snapped James.

They waited while Hilary clambered back into their room, her arms full of paper planes. Then James turned on her. 'What do you think you're doing!' he cried. 'Didn't you read the note?'

'What note?'

Amanda picked out one of the paper planes. It had green writing all over it. '*This* note,' she said.

'I can't read writing,' said Hilary, and she dumped the rest of the paper planes onto James's bed. 'I can only read pictures.'

'Only read *pictures*?' cried James.

'And music,' said Hilary.

There was a shocked pause. 'Well, reading isn't everything,' said Amanda brightly. 'I expect Hilary is far too busy to read – aren't you, Hilary?'

'Not really,' said Hilary, and flopped down on the sofa.

James and Amanda glanced at each other.

'So, er ... what exactly *do* you do?' asked James.

Hilary retrieved a chocolate button that had slipped between the sofa cushions, and popped it into her mouth. 'Not much,' she said.

'But aren't you busy doing lots of ... good deeds?' said Amanda hopefully.

'Good deeds?'

'You know – helping people, and things.'

'Oh yes!' said Hilary, remembering. 'Yes, I'm supposed to do *that*.'

'I thought so,' said Amanda, and she shot a triumphant look at James as though to say, 'See? I told you she's an angel.'

James ignored it and turned to Hilary. 'What sort of help,' he said, 'are you supposed to provide, exactly?'

Hilary promptly sat up straight, put her hand on her heart and began to recite: 'I promise,' she said solemnly, 'to love, honour and obey, for richer or poorer, in sickness and in health, for as long as—'

'Isn't that what people say at weddings?' interrupted James.

'Oh! Yes,' said Hilary. 'It's not that one. It must be "I promise to think of others before myself and do a good turn every—"'

'I know that one!' cried Amanda. 'That's the Brownie Guide Law!'

There was a pause. Then Hilary gave an exasperated sigh. 'I don't *believe* it!' she said. 'I've forgotten it *again,*' and for a moment she looked so dismayed that Amanda felt quite sorry for her.

'If you could read,' said Amanda helpfully, 'you wouldn't have to remember it. You could just carry it round with you on a piece of paper.'

'Mmm,' said Hilary. 'Maybe I'll learn to read when I go to school with you tomorrow.'

'School?' said James.

'Yes,' said Hilary.

James and Amanda looked at each other doubtfully.

'I'm sorry,' said James eventually, 'but you can't come to school with us.'

'Why not?'

'Because you can't! You're not on the register. You wouldn't like it, anyway.'

'I would!'

'You wouldn't!'

'I would – I've *always* wanted to go to school,' protested Hilary. 'In fact, it's my most wanted thing in the *whole world*.'

'Well, I'm sorry,' said James, 'but there isn't any school tomorrow, anyway. It's the weekend. We're going to Beddgelert for a picnic.'

'A picnic?' Hilary clapped her hands excitedly. 'That's my *second* most wanted thing!'

4
The Wonderful Day

Immediately James wished he'd never mentioned the picnic. But Hilary was persistent and, like Amanda said, how could they deny Hilary her second most wanted thing? She would only be bored sitting at home, and surely it couldn't do any harm letting her come with them?

'But what about her wings?' said James.

'We'll disguise them,' said Amanda. 'No one will know.'

James was reluctant, but eventually he agreed to ask their parents if Hilary could come with them – provided her wings didn't show. At least then they would be able to keep an eye on her.

Of course, Mr and Mrs Mulroney were delighted to have the twins' new friend join them on the picnic. 'The more the merrier!' said Mr Mulroney. 'Have we met Hilary before?'

'No,' said James. 'She just moved here.'

'Where from?'

'We don't know,' admitted James.

Mr Mulroney peered at his wife over his glasses. 'Perhaps we should speak to Hilary's parents first,' he said. 'To make sure they don't mind.'

'Oh, they won't mind!' said Amanda airily. 'They'll never even know.'

Mr Mulroney stared at her. 'What do you mean, Amanda?'

'Hilary's parents aren't here,' James said quickly.

'Aren't here? Then where are they?'

'We don't know,' said James. 'We don't like to ask.' This was true enough – and besides, said Amanda later, Hilary was an angel, and angels don't have parents – do they?

'So if Hilary's parents aren't here,' said Mr Mulroney. 'Where is Hilary staying?'

'With friends,' said James.

Mr and Mrs Mulroney exchanged a solemn look. It was their belief that families should stick together. They made a special effort to go on family outings and spend quality time together whenever they could – in fact the Mulroneys spent so much quality time together that the twins sometimes felt it might be nice to have some quality time to themselves for a change.

'Well then,' said Mr Mulroney. 'We'll speak to her friends instead.'

This was clearly a difficulty, since Hilary's 'friends' didn't have their own phone, but eventually it was decided to write them a note instead. James volunteered to deliver it. Out he went, and was back again in a matter of minutes with the news that Hilary's friends had seen the note (he and Amanda had been there while their parents had written it, after all) and that it was all arranged – Hilary would come to the house first thing in the morning and join them on the picnic.

The twins got up especially early on the day of the picnic to disguise Hilary's wings. They found that when Hilary wore Amanda's old brown duffel coat, her wings were hardly noticeable. When the coat was done up the wings were just a bump where her shoulder blades should have been, and when the hood went back it covered the bump quite well. The coat was a bit too big and the sleeves dangled over

Hilary's hands, but the hem of the coat came right down to her ankles and concealed her wingtips perfectly.

'Hooray! Now shoes,' said Amanda.

Hilary sat on the edge of Amanda's bed while they put on her feet a pair of heavy black lace-up shoes that James never wore. Hilary took a few faltering steps around the room, looking down at them.

'Walk properly,' said James. 'Or everyone will think there's something wrong with you.'

'There *is* something wrong with me,' said Hilary, offended. 'I've got a broken wing.'

James looked at her doubtfully, but said nothing.

'And I don't like these shoes,' said Hilary. 'They're too heavy and they rub.'

So they removed James's old black lace-ups, and Hilary sat on the edge of the bed while the twins went back and forth from the wardrobe like assistants in a shoe shop. They fitted Hilary with Wellingtons, then flip-flops, and then the strappy silver dressing-up shoes that used to belong to Mrs Mulroney. But nothing worked.

'These are all right,' said Hilary, mincing round the room in the dressing-up shoes.

But James said they weren't practical. 'Haven't we got anything else?' he asked.

Amanda rooted in the back of the wardrobe once again until she found her old summer sandals, rather flattened.

'It's too cold for sandals,' said James.

'Not if she wears socks.'

So they buckled up the sandals over thick wool socks and told Hilary to take a few test steps.

'They fit!' she cried, and began skipping round the room in her duffel coat, singing, 'I'm going to Beddgelert! I'm going to Beddgelert!'

James looked stern. 'Hilary,' he said.

'You won't forget what we told you, will you?'

'About what?'

'About not drawing attention to yourself.'

But Hilary was already standing on the red chair and opening the skylight – she was going to fly down (as well as could be expected with a broken wing, she said) and ring the doorbell like an ordinary friend.

'Hilary?' said James. 'Did you hear what I said?'

Hilary grinned. 'It's going to be a *wonderful* day,' she said. 'I just *know* it.'

James was not so sure.

It was a long way to Beddgelert. The winding roads made Amanda feel sick, but all the way there Hilary bounced up and down in the back seat and kept up a stream of questions. Mostly it was 'Are we nearly there?' and the answer was always

'Not yet.'

But eventually they *were* there. It was a busy bank holiday weekend and they found the little Welsh town teeming with tourists and day-trippers. The car park was nearly full.

'Here we are,' said Mr Mulroney, pulling into a space. 'Beddgelert! That means "Gelert's Grave" in Welsh, Hilary. Do you know the legend of Gelert? It's quite an interesting story. Gelert …' But Hilary had already jumped out and could be glimpsed running up and down excitedly between the parked cars.

James sighed. 'I'll get her,' he said.

They set off along the riverside. Mr Mulroney stepped out in front with the picnic hamper, and Mrs Mulroney brought up the rear in her walking boots and floppy sunhat. Mrs Mulroney kept fanning herself with the map and saying, 'What a scorcher!' But the warm day didn't seem to bother Hilary at all (despite her duffel coat) and she ran on ahead saying hello to everyone they met.

'Hilary seems to be enjoying herself,' remarked Mrs Mulroney.

'Hmm,' said James uneasily.

At the very end of the path they came to an oak tree with a group of people crowded round it.

'What are they looking at?' asked Hilary.

'Ah,' said Mr Mulroney mysteriously. 'That'll be Gelert's grave.'

'Grave?' said Hilary, and she squeezed her way to the front of the group to peer at a slab of stone set into the grass. There was a lot of writing carved into the stone.

'What does it say?' asked Hilary.

'Well now,' said Mr Mulroney. 'There lies a story.'

'What story?'

The twins slumped; they had heard all their father's stories before. But Mr

Mulroney cleared his throat loudly, and began.

'Many years ago,' he said, and his voice rang out above the gathering, 'Prince Llewelyn had a palace near here. Whenever he came to stay at the palace he went hunting, and he always took with him his faithful hound, Gelert.'

'Hound? What's a hound?' asked Hilary.

'A dog,' said James.

'But on this day,' said Mr Mulroney, 'Gelert wasn't with the hunting party.'

'Why not?' asked Hilary.

'Prince Llewelyn had left Gelert behind to guard his baby son, who was sleeping in his crib.'

'You mean – Gelert was the baby's *guardian*?' cried Hilary.

'Exactly,' said Mr Mulroney.

Hilary clapped her hands delightedly. By this time all the bystanders had fallen quiet and were following the story closely – and none more closely than Hilary.

'When Llewelyn returned from hunting,' continued Mr Mulroney, 'Gelert ran down the palace steps to greet him – and to Llewelyn's horror he saw that the dog's jaws were *covered in blood*.'

Hilary gasped.

'Prince Llewelyn was most alarmed,' said Mr Mulroney. 'He hurried—'

'Was Gelert bleeding?' interrupted Hilary.

'Shush,' said someone in the crowd.

'Llewelyn hurried inside,' repeated Mr Mulroney, 'to find his son. But the crib was empty, and—'

'Empty?' cried Hilary. 'Where was the baby?'

'Shhhh!' said several people at once.

'The baby was gone,' said Mr Mulroney. 'And the blankets and floor were covered in blood.' Here he paused and glanced at Hilary, but Hilary was speechless. 'Well,' he continued, 'Llewelyn put two and two together. He thought that Gelert must have killed his son, so he whipped out his jewelled dagger, raised it high above his head, and plunged it deep into Gelert's side.'

'But—'

'And then, as Gelert gave his dying yelp, there came a child's cry. Llewelyn flung aside the blankets and found his son unharmed, and nearby was the bloody body of a mighty wolf that Gelert had slain.'

There was a horrified silence.

Mr Mulroney looked round at his audience. 'Prince Llewelyn had made a terrible mistake. Gelert had not killed his son – he had killed the wolf to *save* his son.' Mr Mulroney shrugged. 'They say Llewelyn never smiled again. And here, he buried Gelert.'

There was a stillness over the crowd, and even the birds had stopped singing. A distant sheep bleated faintly … and then all of a sudden the silence was shattered by an anguished wail.

'Hilary!' said Mrs Mulroney, shocked.

Everyone turned to look. Hilary's mouth was cawing open and her face was red.

'There, there,' said Mr Mulroney. 'It's only a story.'

'It's not f-f-faaaaaair!' wailed Hilary.

The crowd began to murmur and disperse. Parents were taking their children by the hand and leading them away.

'How about an ice cream?' said Mrs Mulroney brightly. But Hilary just shook her head in a silent wail, and a long dribble swung from the side of her mouth.

'Shut up!' hissed James, glancing around – but Hilary would not be comforted.

'I think we'd better go home,' said Mr Mulroney.

Hilary allowed herself to be led away from Gelert's grave and back along the path. She sniffed miserably all the way to the car, causing everyone they passed to glance at her and shoot dark looks at Mr and Mrs Mulroney. 'It's a *shame*,' said one old lady.

James trailed behind them at a distance, with his hands in his pockets, hoping that no one would notice him.

All the way home Hilary sat slumped in the back seat with her hood up; nothing they could say would cheer her. She just kept sniffling to herself and muttering something about it 'not being easy being a guardian.'

It was a subdued party that arrived outside the Mulroneys' house.

'You go in and put the kettle on,' Mr Mulroney told his wife wearily. 'I'll put the car away.'

But as they all got out Hilary tipped back her hood and turned to Mr Mulroney with a tearstained face. 'Thanks, Mr Mulroney,' she said hoarsely. 'I've had a *wonderful* day.'

5
York Minster

'**I** *love* stories,' said Hilary happily. Ever since the Wonderful Day she had seemed content to sit on the sofa eating chocolate buttons, wearing headphones and listening to Mrs Mulroney's audio romances. She was so quiet that the twins kept forgetting she was there at all, and then were startled when she suddenly yelled out things like, 'Don't do it, Mr Elsewise!' or burst into gleeful laughter.

'Don't you have stories where you come from?' Amanda had asked.

'No,' said Hilary. 'We're not supposed to make things up.'

No stories? The twins looked at Hilary curiously. 'What's it like there?' asked James.

'Where?'

'Wherever it is you come from.'

'Boring,' said Hilary.

'But you must do *something*.'

Hilary considered. 'We sing,' she said. 'Hymns, mostly.'

'Don't you do any dancing?' asked Amanda, who had started taking ballet lessons.

'Sometimes,' said Hilary. 'As long as it's decorous.'

'What's decorous?'

'Not moving your arms and legs too much.'

James and Amanda glanced at each other. Poor Hilary! No wonder she was in no particular hurry to get back – it sounded even worse than school!

'What about games?' asked James. 'Don't you play football?'

'Oh no! They're *far* too old for football.'

'Too old? Aren't there any children there?'

Hilary shook her head. 'Not as many as *here*,' she said. And for a moment she looked almost sad.

Poor Hilary. Amanda supposed it was only to be expected that angels were mainly old people – but it couldn't be much fun for her, could it?

'Well, never mind,' said Amanda eventually. 'You can stay with us for as long as you like – can't she, James?'

But James just glanced at Amanda in annoyance, and said nothing.

Then, one morning as the twins were getting ready for school, Hilary took off the headphones and said, 'What are you doing?'

The twins looked at her.

'We're getting ready for school,' said James. 'What does it look like?'

'You never normally take a water bottle,' said Hilary, whose sharp eyes had missed nothing. 'Or wear your weekend shoes.'

'All right,' admitted James. 'We're not going to school. We're going on a field trip.'

'You're going to a *field*?'

'It's not *in* a field,' explained James. 'We're going to York Minster, a cathedral. It's for our project and we're going on the train.'

'Do they tell stories at York Minster?'

'No,' said James. 'They don't. And even if they did, you still can't come – not after last time.'

'I won't ask questions,' said Hilary. 'They'll never know I'm there.'

'They count,' said James.

'He's right,' said Amanda. 'They do.'

Hilary begged and pleaded, but the twins remained firm, and by the time they left to catch the train Hilary was sulking on the sofa with her headphones on and wouldn't even say goodbye.

'I hope she'll be all right,' said Amanda.

'She'll be fine,' said James.

The train had started hurrying, and the twins looked out onto the backs of unfamiliar houses: gardens coming right down to the railway line, ramshackle sheds and overgrown banks of bindweed with its white trumpet flowers. Gradually the town thinned out and they were passing fields and telegraph poles. 'Lickety-split, lickety-split' went the wheels on the train.

All of a sudden James grabbed Amanda's arm. 'Ow!' said Amanda. 'What?'

James pointed. High above the train and a little way behind, a dark speck was following. It was too big for a bird, too slow for a plane. It looked like a giant hawk, or one of those flying monkeys from *The Wizard of Oz.*

'It can't be,' said Amanda.

But it was.

'She'll never keep up,' said James. 'It's miles to York.'

They watched grimly, but Hilary seemed to be gaining on the train and dropping lower at the same time. Soon they could see her legs kicking like a person doing the crawl, and her white dress billowing about her knees. She was carrying a bundle in her arms. 'Your duffel coat,' said James.

Fortunately no one else in the train seemed to have noticed her, they were too busy squabbling over their lunches. Hilary came lower and lower until the twins lost sight of her behind the train.

'To the back,' said Amanda.

They jumped up and ran shakily down

the aisle, feeling like they were running the wrong way along a conveyor belt with the countryside flashing past in the opposite direction. In the very last carriage there was a window in the door. The tracks stretched behind them – empty. And so was the sky.

'Where did she go?' said Amanda.

In answer there was a sudden *thunk* on the roof of the carriage, and the slap of sandaled feet running down the train.

'She's on the roof!' said James.

6
The Little Monk

When the train pulled in at York, Mrs
Stoke gathered everyone together on
the platform. 'Thirty-three,' she said,
counting heads. 'Good. Follow me! Miss
Evans will bring up the rear.'

The twins looked round for Hilary, but
she was nowhere to be seen. The roof of
the train was clear, and they could see no
brown duffel coat among the crowds.

'Have you two forgotten something?' asked Miss Evans.

'No,' said James, and they hurried to catch up with the others.

There was a guide waiting to meet them outside the west door of the Minster. 'I'm Mr Moffat,' he said. He wore a brown suit and was bald on top with little white tufts of hair over his ears like a koala bear. 'Keep together, everyone. And remember – sshht!' He pressed his fingers to his lips.

It was dim and shady inside York Minster, like a great cave with slanted light coming in through high stained-glass windows. Mr Moffat led the class through the nave, past rows of wooden pews, and waited while everyone gathered round.

'If you look to your left,' said Mr Moffat, 'you will see the organ with its five thousand and three hundred pipes.'

Everyone looked left and saw the organ.

'And if you look to your right,' he

continued, 'you will see the crypt. Here lies the tomb of St Augustus, also known as the Little Monk due to his small stature. He was famous for his bell-ringing.'

Everyone looked right and saw a room with low ceilings and pillars of stone where the bell-ringing monk rested. But Amanda was tugging at James's sleeve. 'Look over there,' she whispered.

James looked. There, standing with a group of Japanese tourists admiring the angels in a stained-glass window, was a small brown duffel-coated figure.

'Keep up, please,' said Mr Moffat.

The twins hurried to catch up with the rest of the class, and when they looked back again Hilary had gone.

'Gather round, everyone,' said Mr Moffat. 'Here we have the rose window. The rose window commemorates the—' He stopped suddenly. 'Excuse me!' he said sharply. 'You there!' And he pointed.

Everyone turned to look. Standing on

tiptoe at the back of the group was a girl in an over-large brown duffel coat.

'Are you with *us*?' asked Mr Moffat.

Hilary looked about. 'Who – me?'

'Yes, you! Where's your group?'

'She's not one of ours,' said Mrs Stoke.

'Shouldn't she be in school?' said Miss Evans.

Everyone stared at Hilary – everyone except James, who was pretending to be interested in something on the ceiling.

'Well, I'm sorry,' said Mr Moffat. 'But you can't join *this* tour.'

'I was only listening!'

'No listening allowed,' said Mr Moffat firmly. 'Unless you're with the group.'

'But—'

'I'm *wait*ing,' sang Mr Moffat.

There was a long silence, then reluctantly Hilary turned and shuffled off. Mr Moffat waited until he thought she was out of earshot. 'That's better,' he said. 'Now then – over here we have the choir stalls.

The acoustics were designed so that—'

'I can hear you!' came a thin cry.

The class looked round to see Hilary standing watching them from the other side of the cathedral.

'As I was saying,' continued Mr Moffat. 'The acoustics—'

'I can still hear you!' This time Hilary was peeping out from behind a pillar, waving at them. The class giggled.

Mr Moffat turned his back on her. 'We'll do the ringing chamber and the bell tower,' he said. He motioned for the class to gather round, and waited until he was sure that Hilary had gone. Then he lowered his voice so that no one could overhear. 'According to legend,' he said, 'the Little Monk used to ring the bells so beautifully that *angels* gathered on the roof to listen.' Mr Moffat paused dramatically and glanced upwards, and all the class glanced upwards too as though they expected to see angels waiting for the bells to ring.

'Where's she gone?' hissed James. Hilary had disappeared.

'This way,' said Mr Moffat. He started up a stone stairway, and the class came after him. Round and round they went, higher and higher. When they were about halfway up the tower, Mr Moffat paused and cleared his throat. 'In the ringing chamber you will see the bell pulls hanging just as they did in fourteen—'

All of a sudden Mr Moffat's voice was drowned out by a noise that sounded like a hundred pots and pans falling from a great height – and it was coming from the ringing chamber up ahead! Mr Moffat gave an outraged yell and leapt on up the stairs.

Crowding into the chamber behind him the class was confronted by a curious sight: a group of tourists were snapping pictures of what looked like a miniature monk swinging on the bell pulls.

'Check it out!' yelled a man in a safari

suit. 'It's a re-enactment by the Little Monk!'

And there was Hilary wearing her duffel coat with the hood up. She was clinging to the bell ropes so that as the bells clanged she sailed up into the belfry and then down again in front of the flashing cameras.

'Hell's bells!' yelled Mr Moffat, rushing forward. 'Stop that!' But Hilary had scuttled up one of the ropes like a monkey and set the bells a-jangling again.

Gradually the bells quietened and the ropes hung still.

'What goes up must come down,' said Miss Evans peering upwards. Then all of a sudden a dark shape came plummeting down towards them and fell to the floor at their feet – thud! Mrs Stoke shrieked and Miss Evans covered her eyes and peeped through her fingers – but it was only Hilary's duffel coat!

So where was Hilary?

While everyone was staring at the coat there came a sudden down-rush of wind, and they all looked up just in time to see something swooping down towards them. Hilary flew straight over the balcony and into the cathedral, and then, like an angel in socks and sandals she circled high above the astonished upturned faces. Once, twice round she went, then she dived straight downwards with her white dress snapping and cracking round her calves. People below screamed and took cover between the pews, but Hilary shot straight out through the West door and disappeared.

There was a moment's silence and then everyone began talking loudly. When no one was looking, Amanda picked up Hilary's duffel coat and stuffed it into her backpack.

Soon the police arrived. They said they suspected that the 'Little Monk' stunt was

some sort of student prank and everyone had to be questioned before they could leave. So the class missed the early train, and their dinner, and James never did get to draw the tomb of St Augustus for his project – all because of Hilary. 'What did she think she was *playing at*?' he said. 'I thought she had a broken wing?'

'She doesn't like being left behind,' Amanda told him.

James just grunted. He didn't say another word all the way home.

It was eight o'clock by the time they got back and they found Hilary sleeping soundly on the sofa as though she had never left it. 'Wake up,' said James, shaking her by the shoulder.

'Ow!' said Hilary. 'Mind my wing.' Then she turned over and fell asleep again.

'Ow, nothing,' snapped James. 'There's nothing wrong with that wing! Isn't it time you went home?'

7
The Angel Gabriel

'I don't think she's got a broken wing at all,' said James the following morning, while he and Amanda were brushing their teeth. 'It's just an excuse.'

'An excuse for what?'

'For not going home,' said James. 'She likes it here too much.'

'Don't be silly,' said Amanda.

'Well, it can't be much fun singing carols with a lot of old people, can it?'

'Hymns,' corrected Amanda. 'And she isn't here because she *likes* it. She's here to *help* someone.'

'Help someone! What makes you think she's going to *help* anyone?'

Amanda sighed. 'That's what angels *do*,' she said. 'Especially *guardian* angels – they help people.'

James just spat in the sink and said, 'There's no such thing as angels.' And before Amanda could say anything else he had marched out of the bathroom.

But even James had to admit that Hilary had been on her best behaviour lately. While the twins were at school, she busied herself with drawing and jigsaws. She kept as quiet as a mouse so that Mr and Mrs Mulroney wouldn't suspect that she was there, and she was always so pleased to see the twins when they got home that it was hard to remain angry with her. Also, Christmas was coming, which always put

James in a good mood. At school they were making paper snowflakes to decorate the classroom – and best of all they had started practising for the Christmas play.

'I play a shepherd,' James told Hilary proudly. 'The one who speaks.' He shook his script at Amanda. 'Here – you be Gabriel.'

Amanda took the script and found the place where the Angel Gabriel comes in. 'DO NOT BE AFRAID,' she read.

'Wait a minute,' said James, who was putting his dressing gown on over his clothes. 'You've got to fly in from the right, and surprise us while we tend our flocks.'

Amanda sighed, and went to conceal herself behind the curtain.

'BEHOLD,' cried James, falling to his knees and raising his arms dramatically. 'THE ANGEL GABRIEL!'

Amanda came running out from behind the curtain, flapping her arms. 'DO NOT BE AFRAID!' she said. 'I'M HERE TO—'

'Gabriel?' interrupted Hilary. 'There's a part in your play for *Angel* Gabriel? With *wings*?'

James sighed and let down his arms. 'Percy's playing the angel,' he said.

'Does Percy have wings?'

'His mum's making them,' said Amanda. 'Out of cardboard. She's sticking feathers on and—'

'Cardboard!' cried Hilary. 'Cardboard's no good. Everyone will *know* they're not real.'

'It's a play,' said James, wearily. 'It doesn't *have* to be real.'

'He'll never get off the ground!'

'He doesn't *have* to,' cried James. 'They lower him on a wire.'

'A *wire*?' Hilary shook her head. 'I don't think Gabriel would allow *that*,' she said.

'It's all pretend,' explained Amanda. 'That's why it's called a play. You'll see.'

But Hilary was not convinced. She went to sit on the sofa with her arms

folded, and while the twins practised
James' lines, she watched them
thoughtfully.

By opening night Hilary knew the script
better than they did. She had been invited
to accompany Mr and Mrs Mulroney to the
school hall to watch the play, provided she
behaved herself. 'But remember to keep
quiet,' James told her, 'and don't clap until
the end.'

'She's more excited than the twins,'
remarked Mrs Mulroney. 'And she's not
even in it!'

Hilary just smiled, and said nothing.

The play was sold out. The gymnasium
had been filled with rows of chairs, the
lights dimmed, and heavy red curtains
drawn across the stage. While the orchestra
tuned up at the front (Amanda was playing
the violin and she waved her bow at Mr
and Mrs Mulroney) all the parents took

their seats. Eventually the chatter and the rustling of programmes subsided, and with a drum roll the curtains went back.

'It's a quiet night,' came a voice from the wings. 'Three shepherds tend their flocks.'

The music teacher lifted his baton and the orchestra started up like a rusty machine. Then, onto the stage came three small shepherds, quite close together. All of them were wearing dressing gowns and carrying walking sticks, and had tea towels on their heads.

'Which one is James?' whispered Mr Mulroney.

'The one with the poppies on his tea towel,' replied Mrs Mulroney.

The shepherds stopped in the middle of the stage, and waited for their sheep (seven of the younger children) who came shuffling out after them on all fours with their woolly white tails and ears joggling.

'Excuse me,' whispered Hilary.

'Where are you going?' hissed Mr
Mulroney.

'It's my cue,' said Hilary.

'What?'

'… going to the loo,' said Hilary, and
she edged past Mr and Mrs Mulroney and
hurried out through a side door.

Now a yellow moon was rising on the
back wall, and the light was dimming. The
shepherds put down their crooks and lay
on the floor, and the sheep all huddled up
together. The shepherd that was James
yawned loudly and smacked his lips, and
the audience tittered. Then all of a sudden
a very bright light shone down on the
stage and the shepherds sat up, blinking
and shading their eyes. 'BEHOLD,' cried
the shepherd who was James, raising his
arms dramatically. 'THE ANGEL GABRIEL!'

James waited with his arms raised.
Nothing happened.

'BEHOLD!' cried James again. 'IT'S THE

ANGEL GABRIEL!'

Still nothing happened. Then all of a sudden a mysterious winged figure wearing socks and sandals and a black eye mask launched herself onto the stage. She landed heavily and staggered a bit, but recovered and stood facing the astonished shepherds and their startled sheep.

'DO NOT BE AFRAID!' said Hilary, flinging wide her arms.

There was a moment's hesitation, then, as one, the sheep clambered to their feet and ran shrieking off the stage. Two of the shepherds followed, letting their crooks clatter to the floor.

'DO NOT BE AFRAID!' said Hilary again. But it was too late – they had gone. Only James remained on stage. Hilary turned and beamed at him. 'I AM THE ANGEL GABRIEL,' she said.

The lone shepherd glared at the Angel Gabriel.

'I,' said Hilary, a little more loudly this

time, 'AM THE ANGEL GABRIEL!'

'I HEARD YOU THE FIRST TIME!' yelled James.

The audience burst into laughter, and the shepherd that was James went very red – but the Angel Gabriel wasn't fazed. She waited until the laughter had died down, then she turned to the glowering shepherd.

'I'M HERE TO TELL YOU,' she said loudly, 'THAT A *KING IS BORN TONIGHT!*'

The shepherd that was James scowled and said nothing.

'FOLLOW YONDER STAR,' cried Hilary, and with one arm flung out towards the imaginary star, she sprinted across the stage, spread her wings and leapt out over the audience. She circled the room once, twice, then disappeared into the lofty darkness of the gymnasium.

There was a moment's silence, then everyone began to talk at once.

'All done with mirrors, of course,' said Mr Mulroney.

Hilary returned after the interval, a little flushed and out of breath.

'Where have you been?' asked Mrs Mulroney. 'You missed the best bit!'

'Never mind,' said Hilary, hiding a small smile. 'You can tell me later,' and she settled back contentedly to watch the second half.

But after the spectacular appearance of the Angel Gabriel, the play fell rather flat. The orchestra seemed distracted, and whenever the shepherds appeared they came on brandishing their crooks like weapons and glancing at the ceiling. The sheep refused to appear at all.

Hilary enjoyed it though. 'BEHOLD THE ANGEL GABRIEL!' she shouted in the car on the way home. 'Mrs Mulroney,' she said. 'Tell us again about the Angel Gabriel. Was it the best part?'

Mrs Mulroney admitted that the Angel Gabriel had been very good indeed. Everyone had loved it.

Everyone, that is, but James. He sat sulking in the back, his face turned towards the passing night. 'What's the matter, James?' asked his mother.

'Nothing,' said James.

'Tell us again, Mr Mulroney,' persisted Hilary. 'What did it look like when the Angel Gabriel came down and—'

'Shut up!' yelled James.

'James!' said Mr Mulroney, shocked. 'That's enough!' He turned to his wife. 'I think,' he said darkly, 'we might have a *prima donna* in the back seat.'

James scowled and slumped back into his corner, and all the way home nothing more was said.

No one could explain the angel. Everyone supposed that someone's relative had pulled the stunt – perhaps someone who worked in the film industry.

'I just feel sorry for Percy,' said Amanda. 'He still hasn't found his wings.'

But James was furious. Hilary had ruined *everything*, he said, and he'd never forgive her. 'There's nothing wrong with that wing,' he grumbled. 'When is she going home again – that's what I want to know!'

8
Hilary's Treat

The following day it rained. Hilary and the twins were up in the attic, painting. That is, Hilary and Amanda were painting – James was sitting by himself at the corner table, colouring in. He hadn't said a word to Hilary all morning, and was stippling vigorously with the red pencil.

'I don't know why he's so upset,' said Hilary. 'It was much better with me in it.

Much more *authentic*.'

'He says you made him look stupid.'

'He would have looked even stupider talking to someone on the end of a piece of string.'

'Wire,' corrected Amanda.

'Wire, then,' said Hilary. She was thoughtful for a moment, then she leant towards Amanda confidentially. 'I know the *real* reason he's upset,' she said.

James stopped dotting and looked up from his corner. 'Why is that?'

'You're jealous,' said Hilary.

'Jealous!' shouted James. 'I'm not jealous! Why would I be jealous of *you*?'

Hilary smiled gently. 'Because I can fly,' she said. 'And you can't.'

James made an exasperated sound, and started dotting again.

'But you needn't worry,' continued Hilary, 'because I'm going to make it up to you.'

James paused.

'Make it up to him?' said Amanda.

'Yes! I'm going to *treat* you – both of you.'

'Treat us? How?'

Hilary smiled mysteriously. 'I'll give you a clue,' she said, and she put her arms out and started swooping round the room making a noise like an engine.

'What's that – a plane?' said James.

'No.'

'Superman?'

'No.'

'I give up,' said James.

Hilary stopped swooping. 'We're going *flying,* silly!'

There was a long, uncertain silence.

'What's the matter?' said Hilary. 'Don't you want to?'

'Yes, but … how?'

'I'll carry you. We'll use a sheet,' said Hilary. 'It'll be just like when the stork delivers babies.'

'You'd drop us,' said James. 'We'd be

too heavy.'

'I wouldn't drop you!' cried Hilary, offended. 'I'm good at looking after people! Anyway, the difficult bit is taking off. Once you're in the air it's OK.'

James considered. 'What about your broken wing?'

Hilary rolled her shoulders experimentally. 'It's much better now,' she said.

James looked doubtful.

'Come on, James,' coaxed Amanda. 'Let's try it.'

'Well …' said James. 'All right then – as long as nobody sees us.'

Amanda clapped her hands and jumped up and down. 'When shall we go?'

'Tonight,' said Hilary. 'After dark.'

That night, when all the lights had gone out downstairs and the rest of the house was quiet, they stripped the sheet from James' bed and spread it on the floor. Then the twins, all dressed and ready, stepped onto it and waited for instructions.

'Right,' said Hilary, looking them up and down. 'Now take all your clothes off.'

'What?' cried the twins.

'Weight,' explained Hilary. 'We need to get your weight down.'

'Well, I'm not going with nothing on,' said Amanda, stepping back onto the carpet.

'I'm sorry,' said Hilary. 'But I can't carry any extras. Think how heavy jeans get when they're wet.'

'They're not going to get wet!'

'They will if it rains. And look at your shoes – and those buttons. They all add up.'

The twins considered.

'I'm keeping my shoes on,' said James. 'I don't care what you say.'

'All right,' said Hilary. 'But you'll have to lose the rest.'

There was an anxious silence. 'I know!'

said Amanda suddenly, and she went to ferret in her underwear drawer. She brought out something pink with yellow flowers on it and shook it at the others. 'Swimsuits!'

Hilary took the garment in her hand and weighed it thoughtfully. 'All right,' she said.

'We'll freeze,' protested James. But Hilary had made her mind up, so eventually James went behind the curtain to put on his trunks. He came back a moment later with his arms folded across his chest, looking very thin and very white, and wearing his school lace-ups without any socks.

Hilary seemed satisfied. She even let them wear their woolly hats to keep warm. Then, as quietly as they could, they climbed out onto the roof and laid the sheet on the tiles. It was a cold, clear night, and the moon made everything look like a black-and-white photograph. The twins could see their breath on the air.

'Sit in the middle,' said Hilary.

The twins sat down side by side and waited, shivering with cold and excitement, while Hilary brought the corners of the sheet up around them and made a knot. 'We'll never get off the ground,' muttered James, his teeth chattering.

'Ready?' said Hilary.

'Ready,' said the twins, their woolly-hatted heads poking out at the top.

Hilary looped her arms under the knot and tested it. Then she spread her wings and with one strong wingbeat she was in the air above them; a second wingbeat and the twins felt the sheet straining – and on the third wingbeat they clutched each other and lifted off the tiles.

'Help!' yelped James. (Later he told them he had just said 'Well!', but it certainly sounded a lot like 'Help!' at the time.)

'We're flying!' squealed Amanda.

The rooftops fell away below. From

above, their house looked strange: the garden smaller, the garage at an unexpected angle. And as they climbed higher they recognized other streets laid out below them, and the houses of neighbours, and the corner where the school bus stopped.

It was quiet up there except for the sound of Hilary's wings beating above them, and the rush of wind past their ears.

'Are we heavy?' called James.

'No!' croaked Hilary. Her bare feet were kicking briskly, like a swimmer doing the crawl.

The ground was even further away now, and the twins could see the lights of cars moving slowly along the roads. Hilary flew on.

'Where are we going?' called Amanda.

Hilary just grunted.

They passed over a glittering black stretch of water towards another cluster of lights. 'Look, it's Rhos-on-Sea,' said James, pointing.

They seemed to be getting lower.

'Are we going down?' called Amanda.

'Umph!' said Hilary, kicking ever quicker.

They were definitely dropping. Now they could see individual houses and parked cars. Soon they could see into lighted bedroom windows. Amanda saw a man drawing the curtains.

'Are we going to land?' called James.

Now they were level with the streetlights; now with the upstairs bedrooms. Now they were flying down the middle of the road – and they were still dropping.

'I don't think we should land here,' remarked James.

Hilary was still beating her wings and kicking valiantly.

'We might as well be walking!' said James, for now they were barely skimming

the surface of the road. A moment later they touched down with a bump and found themselves sprawled on the road in their swimsuits.

'Ow!' said Amanda, nursing her knee.

James bundled up the sheet and glanced about angrily.

'Why did you put us down here?' he said. 'Anyone could see us!'

'C-couldn't help it,' gasped Hilary. She was staggering about in the middle of the road, taking rasping great breaths, and clutching her chest. 'Too heavy. Must have been the shoes.'

'I *knew* it,' James said bitterly. 'Now what do we do?'

'We're grounded,' said Amanda.

And so they were. It was a cold night, and woolly hats aren't much help when you're wearing nothing but your swimsuit and school shoes. James wrapped the sheet round Amanda and himself and they stood there, teeth chattering, wondering what to do.

'I'll be all right in a minute,' said Hilary. 'I just need a high place to take off from.'

'Great,' said James sarcastically. 'How about we knock on someone's door and say, "Excuse me, can we just use your roof for a minute?"'

'If we could only find a tree …' said Amanda. But it was one of those new housing estates where there are only small spiky bushes and flimsy saplings.

'We'll just have to turn around and walk back,' said James. 'Until we see something.' And he and Amanda set off walking, wrapped in the sheet. It felt like the time they went trick-or-treating, dressed as a pantomime horse, only this time they were both the head.

'Wait for me!' cried Hilary.

So off they went – but none of them had noticed the curtains twitching in the house across the road, or the lady with

horn-rimmed glasses peering out after them
with a telephone pressed against her ear.

9
Home Again, Hilary

'Which way now?' asked Amanda. They had walked what seemed like miles and seen nothing higher than a post box, and now they found themselves on a busy highway with cars whizzing past at lightning speed. As each car went by, the trio were illuminated in the headlights; the twins shrouded in James's grubby white sheet, and Hilary with her white dress and her long white wings.

'Let's keep walking,' said Amanda. 'Maybe we'll pass one of those phones where you can call for help.'

So on they went, picking their way along the hard shoulder, with James muttering something like, 'Great treat, Hilary. Thanks a lot.'

It's only when you're walking on them that you realize how long highways can be, and how boring. There were no landmarks up ahead to show them they were making any progress. It was like being in the desert – deserts get cold at night, as well.

'Let's run to keep warm,' said James.

So the twins set off jogging, with the sheet wrapped round them. They were just getting into the rhythm of it – left-right, left-right – when they heard the sudden swoosh of tyres on gravel and turned round to see a car pulling off the road behind them. They stood blinking in the flashing blue lights as the door opened and the dark silhouette of a policeman got out.

'Hold it right there, kids,' he said.

And of course, they should have done just that. But when you're out in the middle of the night wearing only a sheet and your swimsuit and your parents think you're still tucked up in bed, and when one of you has wings, you might be silly enough to do the first thing that comes to mind.

'Run!' said James.

So they did.

PC Footit frowned and switched on his radio.

'569 to Central Control,' he said.

'Go ahead, 569,' came the crackling reply.

'I've found the kids,' said PC Footit. 'They're heading down the A55. I'm pursuing on foot.'

He switched off the radio and started after them.

The twins stumbled along the hard shoulder with Hilary right behind them, but they couldn't keep running forever. James was limping from a stone in his shoe, and Amanda was beginning to wheeze. Then, just as they thought they would have to stop and turn themselves in, Hilary gave a cry. 'Look!' she said. 'A bridge!' and with a sudden spurt of energy she sprinted down the road, spread her wings, and took off.

'Wait for us!' cried Amanda.

Not far behind them PC Footit was fumbling for his radio. '569 approaching the footbridge,' he gasped, 'in pursuit of … of …' PC Footit stopped short and his mouth fell open. From where he stood he saw one of the small white figures lift clean up off the ground, sail through the air and alight on the top of the bridge.

'569?' came a far-off voice. 'Arc you there? 569?'

But from PC Footit's end there was just a static crackle in reply.

Hilary stood shivering on top of the bridge with her arms folded across her chest. 'Hurry up!' she shouted to the twins. Then she noticed something strange – in the distance were the flashing blue lights of another police car. It was heading towards the bridge very slowly, and backed up behind it was a long line of traffic. That was odd. Then, turning round, Hilary saw a second police car approaching from the opposite direction – and it too had a line of traffic behind it. The cars came to a stop directly under the bridge, blocking both lanes, and out of each police car jumped four police officers.

'What's going on?' gasped the twins, joining Hilary at the railings.

'I don't know,' said Hilary.

'THIS IS PC BAILEY,' shouted one of the officers through a loudspeaker. 'STAY

RIGHT WHERE YOU ARE!'

'I think he means us,' said Amanda.

Now people were getting out of the cars behind. They were slamming doors and coming down to the front to see what the hold-up was all about. Pretty soon there was quite a crowd of onlookers jostling for position at the front.

'Don't do it!' someone called.

'Do what?' said Hilary.

'Come on, Hilary. Let's go,' said James. He and Amanda shrugged off the sheet, spread it out and sat down in the middle. Hilary pulled up the corners and began to knot them.

Below, the officers were trying to get everyone back in their cars, but the crowd seemed reluctant to go, and there was a rising babble of protest. 'YOU ON THE BRIDGE!' yelled PC Bailey. 'DON'T DO ANYTHING RASH!'

'Rash?' said Hilary. 'What's he talking about?'

'Hilary!' shrieked Amanda. 'Quick!'

Hilary looked round. Huffing and puffing and edging his way along the railings towards them was PC Footit.

'Hurry!' cried James.

'Easy now,' said PC Footit.

Hilary tested the knot; then she looped her arms under it.

'Quick!' squealed Amanda.

Hilary spread her wings, and for one magical moment she looked from below like a marble angel, pale against the night sky. The onlookers gasped. Then with a single wing-beat she rose into the air, the sheet straining below her. With another wing-beat the heavy load was airborne. With one more beat of her wings she would have cleared the railings and lifted the twins up and out of reach – but too late, as PC Footit lunged forward and seized James by his dangling foot.

'Let go!' cried James.

Hilary grunted and flapped, but PC

Footit held on bravely. Then, when it seemed that neither would give way and that James's foot was sure to come off, there was a sound like something coming unstuck, and Hilary sprang free.

'We're away!' she cried.

'No we're not,' wailed James. 'I've *left my shoe behind*!'

And there on the bridge stood PC Footit, gazing up at them with his mouth open and holding James's school shoe in one hand.

There was nothing that Hilary could do but head for home. From the air they could see that they had already walked most of the way back, and that the Mulroneys' house was only a couple of streets away. Before long they had landed gently on their own rooftop and sneaked back in through the skylight.

'Well!' said Hilary, shaking the grit out of James's sheet and putting it back on his

bed. 'All's well that ends well.'

'It didn't end well!' cried James. 'I lost my shoe! How am I going to explain that?'

'Tell your mother it fell off,' said Hilary, 'and you had to leave it behind.'

James made an exasperated sound and climbed into bed.

'Or tell her that somebody took it,' said Hilary.

James didn't answer, but could be heard grunting and muttering, trying to get the rest of the grit out of his sheets.

'Good night, then,' said Hilary.

'Good night,' said Amanda.

'I'm sorry about the shoe, James.' There was no answer, so Hilary tried again. 'I didn't know you'd be so heavy,' she said. 'I thought … I thought …'

'You *didn't* think!' shouted James, throwing back the covers and sitting up. 'That's why everything you do goes wrong!'

'But I only wanted to treat you.'

'*Treat* us?' cried James. 'I'll tell you what would treat us! If you went home again – now *that* would be a treat!'

10
Hilary Goes to School

There was a shocked silence. Then
Hilary let out a sob and flung her face
into the pillow.

'He didn't mean it,' said Amanda.

'Yes he did,' said Hilary in a muffled
voice.

'Tell her, James,' pleaded Amanda. 'Tell
her you didn't mean it.'

James sighed. 'I didn't mean it,' he said.

But Hilary didn't say another word all night, and when the twins were ready to leave for school the following morning she was still lying on the sofa with her face pressed into the pillows.

'Come on, Hilary,' said Amanda. 'James doesn't *really* want you to go. Neither of us do.' She shook Hilary's shoulder gently. 'We've got to go to school now. Here – I'm leaving you my chocolate buttons.'

Hilary just mumbled something unintelligible and shrugged off Amanda's hand.

'Come *on*,' said James. 'We're going to miss the bus.' So, reluctantly, Amanda left her chocolate buttons on the arm of the sofa and they headed down the stairs.

'Do you think she'll be all right?' asked Amanda.

'Of course she will,' said James.

As soon as she heard the front door bang, Hilary sat up, put on her socks and sandals, and picked up her duffel coat. Then she dragged across the big red chair, opened the skylight, and climbed out. She stood on the roof for a minute or two and waited until the school bus had pulled away and was heading down the road. Then she folded her duffel coat over her arm, spread her wings, and took off after it.

There wasn't much traffic on the roads this early, and the school bus throttled loudly along, making lots of turns and stopping every now and again to let more children on. Hilary followed its meandering route and eventually, drifting up towards her on the breeze, came the clamour of the playground. Hilary's heart leapt. So *this* was where James and Amanda spent their day. It sounded as though they were all having an enormous party! Hilary frowned. Why should *she* have to stay at home alone while everyone else was down there having fun? It wasn't fair – she *never* got to have fun. Well, today Hilary would go to school like all the other children – and this time no one would stop her. With a flutter of excitement she circled the school once, twice, then started to descend …

Hilary touched down out of sight behind some bins that smelled of potato peelings and old pears. She put on her duffel coat and smoothed her hair, then she took a deep breath and stepped out from behind the bins. At once she was confronted by a yard full of children all rushing about and yelling to one another.

'Hello!' said Hilary, waving shyly. 'Yoo-hoo! Can I …' But all of a sudden there was a deafening jangle and everyone started running for the doors.

'Hey!' yelled Hilary. 'Wait!' She was buffeted left and right as people surged past. 'Where's everyone going?' she wailed. But no one answered, and a moment later Hilary found herself alone in the playground as the last boy ran up the steps, and in. The door banged after him.

Hilary hesitated. She took one last glance round the deserted playground and then she too hurried up the steps after the others.

Hilary found herself in a long empty corridor with doors down either side, and from behind the doors came the chatter of activity and the sound of chairs scraping back. The doors all had glass panels at the top, so Hilary went up to the first one, stood on tiptoe, and looked inside.

A woman with glasses on a gold chain was reading aloud. Hilary tried to hear what sort of story it was – but caught only words like 'subtraction' and 'division'. Hilary had missed the beginning anyway, and beginnings are always crucial. Still – there were plenty more rooms to try.

In the next room Hilary could see children with their heads down, scribbling in their books. It didn't look very interesting, so Hilary moved on. She was just about to peep through a third window, when a door opened further down the corridor and a lady came out.

'Hello,' said the lady, looking at Hilary in surprise. 'Why aren't you in class?'

'I'm choosing,' Hilary told her.

'Choosing?' said the teacher, whose name was Mrs Murray. 'You can't *choose*. Who's your regular teacher?'

'I don't know,' said Hilary. 'It's my first day.'

'First day! Has no one shown you where to go?'

'No.'

'Dear me. What's your name?'

'Hilary.'

'Hilary what?'

'Hilary nothing.'

'Hilary Nothing,' said Mrs Murray slowly. 'Hmm ... it doesn't *sound* familiar. Never mind. Come with me.'

She went to a nearby door, knocked

twice, and entered.

Hilary found herself standing before a sea of curious faces, all turned towards her. There was a lady at the front with chopsticks in her hair.

'It's Hilary's first day,' said Mrs Murray. 'Do you mind if I leave her with you for a moment, Miss Lewis?'

'Not at all,' said Miss Lewis, and she smiled at Hilary. 'There's an empty seat over there. James will look after you. Won't you, James?'

Hilary looked around and to her surprise she saw James and Amanda staring at her from the back of the class. She waved cheerfully, and made her way over.

'What are *you* doing here?' whispered Amanda.

'Coming to school,' said Hilary.

'You can't just *come to school*,' hissed James. 'You're not even on the register!'

'Quiet, please!' said Miss Lewis,

glancing at James. 'Today we are doing still-life drawing of fruit.' With a flourish she unveiled a small table at the front of the class on which sat an orange, a plum, and a banana. 'Paints or pastels, whichever you prefer. Hands up if you have any questions.'

At once everyone got up and started rummaging in the drawers and cupboards. Hilary looked round, expectantly. 'Isn't this exciting!' she exclaimed, and off she went to find some paints.

'She's gone too far this time,' James said bitterly. 'She's going to get us *all* in trouble.'

'Just ignore her,' said Amanda.

James scowled, but he got out his pencil and began sharpening it.

Soon Hilary returned with her supplies and she sat down and started mixing colours and tinkling brushes loudly in her water jar. Then she stood back to look at the fruit and made some sort of measurement by squinting through her fingers.

James tried to ignore her. He shielded his paper with his arm and started drawing. He drew very carefully, with a lot of rubbing out when things went wrong. His picture was very small and very neat, and right in the middle of the paper.

Meanwhile, Hilary had started painting with big, sweeping strokes, getting as much paint as possible on her brush. Every now and again she would stand back to get a better look, then dab more colour here and there.

'Very dramatic, Hilary,' said Miss Lewis.

Hilary gave a blue grin. She had put the wrong end of the paintbrush in her mouth by mistake.

'And what about Amanda?' said Miss Lewis.

Amanda was shading carefully with yellow pastels. 'Lovely! And James?'

James, who'd been concealing his sketch

in the crook of his arm, now had to show it. Hilary got up, too, and came to see. There was a pause.

'Very … tidy,' said Miss Lewis.

'Aren't you going to colour it in?' said Hilary.

'No,' snapped James. 'I'm not.'

Miss Lewis moved on. Hilary went back to her painting, humming softly. James returned to his sketch. For a while, all was peaceful and the only sounds were the sounds of paintbrushes tinkling in water jars and pencils scratching gently. But before long Hilary grew bored. 'Finished!' she said, and she got up and started wandering between the desks with her paintbrush in her hand.

'*Now* what's she doing?' muttered James.

Hilary was going round the classroom peering over people's shoulders and making comments about their work. 'You've missed a bit,' she said to Jeremy

Short, taking her brush and dabbing at his picture.

'Oi!' said Jeremy.

James kept his head down and tried to concentrate on his drawing. He was working on a very delicate part at the top of the orange – that little green star where it joins to the branch.

All of a sudden he felt Hilary looking over his shoulder.

'What's that?' she asked.

'What's what?' said James.

'That,' said Hilary, pointing with her brush. And that's when it happened. A big blob of red paint chose that very moment to drop off the end of Hilary's paintbrush and land right in the middle of James's picture. It was such a big blob, and James's sketch was so small, that it nearly blotted out the whole thing.

For a moment neither James nor Hilary moved. Then all of a sudden James leapt to his feet and made a grab for Hilary's paintbrush. 'Give me that!' he roared.

'James!' cried Miss Lewis, hurrying towards them.

There was a brief struggle. 'Have it, then!' said Hilary, and she let go suddenly. But the moment she let go of the brush it flicked back towards James and red paint spattered all over his face. He let out a yell.

'James!' said Miss Lewis. 'Control yourself!'

'It's her!' cried James. 'She does this all the time!'

'Does what all the time?'

But James couldn't answer. He was wiping his mouth with the back of his sleeve.

Miss Lewis sighed. 'I'm disappointed in you, James,' she said. 'What sort of impression is Hilary going to get on her first day here?'

'I don't care,' said James, dcfiantly. '*She shouldn't be here at all!*'

There was a shocked pause.

'Right,' said Miss Lewis. 'That's enough. I want you to go to the headmaster's office straight away, James, and tell him what you've done. Go on!'

Amanda could only watch in dismay as James threw down the brush and stalked out of the classroom, slamming the door behind him.

11
The Confession

James knocked softly on the
headmaster's door.

'Come in,' said Mr Williams.

James had never been in the
headmaster's office before. It was like a
room in a house, with a big wooden desk
and a sofa and a plant in one corner.
Above the fireplace was a picture of a
yacht.

Mr Williams looked up. 'James
Mulroney,' he said, with some surprise.

'What brings you here?'

'Miss Lewis sent me,' James replied, looking at the floor.

'Did she, now? And why was that?'

James mumbled something.

'I beg your pardon?'

James mumbled something else.

'I see,' said Mr Williams. He pressed the tips of his fingers together and regarded James thoughtfully. 'I think you'd better start from the beginning.'

But before James could begin, Mr Williams's phone rang. 'Excuse me a moment,' said Mr Williams.

James waited.

'Duffel coat?' said Mr Williams. 'Says her name is Nothing? No, she's not with me.' He put down the phone and looked at James. 'Wait here,' he said, and he got up and went out, shutting the door behind him.

James looked around the room. He was just wondering whether it would be all right if he sat on the sofa when the door opened again, and in came Hilary.

'All right,' she said. 'Where is he?'

'You can't come in here!' cried James.

'Don't worry,' said Hilary. 'I've come to confess. I'm going to tell him it was all my fault – even though it wasn't.' She went and sat in Mr Williams's chair with her sandals up on the edge of the desk and her hands behind her head. 'I'll take *all* the blame,' she told him, sounding like one of the heroes from Mrs Mulroney's audio romances. 'I'll be a martyr.'

'A martyr?' cried James. 'What are you talk—'

Just then the door opened and in came Mr Williams. 'Hello!' he said. 'And who have we here?'

Hilary removed her sandals from the edge of the desk, stood up and held out a hand. 'How do you do?' she said. 'I'm Hilary.'

There was a pause. 'Hilary?' said Mr

Williams. He took her hand and shook it. 'I've heard about you.'

'Yes,' said Hilary. 'I'm here to confess. Please take a seat.'

Mr Williams sat down on the sofa and reached inside his jacket pocket. Then he hesitated. 'Excuse me a moment, I need to make a phone call.'

'Of course,' said Hilary.

Mr Williams took out his phone and dialled. 'Yes,' he said. 'She's in my office. Right. Goodbye.' And he put the phone away again.

'Sit down, James,' said Hilary.

When they were both seated Hilary sat back down in the headmaster's chair and folded her arms on the edge of the table. 'There's been a misunderstanding,' she said.

'There has?' said Mr Williams.

'Yes. It was all my fault.'

'What was?'

'Everything,' said Hilary.

'I see,' said Mr Williams. 'Perhaps you'd better start from the beginning.'

But before Hilary could begin, the door flew open and in came Mrs Murray, followed closely by Miss Lewis. 'That's her!' said Mrs Murray, pointing.

'She's not on our register,' said Miss Lewis breathlessly. 'I've checked. And I've spoken to St Mary's and to Highbridge. They don't have a Nothing there, either.'

Despite himself, James gave a snort of laughter.

'And what's the matter with you?' asked Mrs Murray.

'Nothing!'

'All right, young lady, the game is up,' said Mr Williams sternly. 'What's your real name?'

'Hilary!' said Hilary, bewildered.

'And what school do you go to?'

'I don't go to school!'

'Come, come,' said Mr Williams. 'Everyone goes to school.'

'I don't,' said Hilary.

Mr Williams frowned.

'Ask her where she lives!' demanded Mrs Murray.

'Telephone her parents!' said Miss Lewis.

But it was no use. Hilary could provide neither an address nor a telephone number, and when they asked her where she'd come from she just pointed out of the window and said, 'from over there'. Mr Williams sighed and took out his phone again. 'I'm afraid you leave me no option,' he said. 'If you won't tell the truth I shall have to call the—'

'Wait!' said James, jumping to his feet. 'It's true! She doesn't have a telephone. And she doesn't go to school, either.'

The teachers exchanged disbelieving glances.

'And why,' said Mr Williams, 'might that be?'

'Because ...' said James. 'Because ...'

Everybody waited.

'Because ... um ...'

'Because *what?*' said Mrs Murray.

James hesitated. 'Because she's an *angel,*' he said bravely.

For a moment everyone just stared at him. Then Mrs Murray blinked. 'I don't care *how* well behaved she is,' she said. 'She still has to go to school.' She turned to Mr Williams. 'Let's look inside her coat,' she said. 'Maybe her name is on the label.'

'Good idea!' said Mr Williams. And all three teachers began to advance.

'Run, Hilary!' shouted James.

Hilary saw a gap and made a dash for the door, but Mr Williams was too quick. He grabbed her by the hood.

'Hold still,' said Mrs Murray, squeezing her fingers down the back of Hilary's collar. But this only made Hilary shriek and wriggle and shout that they were tickling.

'Buttons, Lewis!' said Mr Williams.

Hilary struggled, but she was no match

for the three of them. One by one her buttons came undone and all of a sudden Mr Williams found he was holding an empty duffel coat by the hood. And there was Hilary – standing before them in her long white dress with her long white wings standing out behind her. Her feathers were ruffled. All three teachers suddenly became very still, and their mouths fell open.

'I think you'd better go,' said James to Hilary. And he went and opened the window for her.

'Thank you for having me,' said Hilary. None of the teachers answered. Hilary stepped up on the headmaster's chair and climbed out through the window. She spread her wings and rose up into the sky and before long she was just a small dark speck against the clouds – then gone completely.

A moment passed. Mrs Murray sat down heavily in the headmaster's chair and asked for a glass of water. Miss Lewis rubbed her temples and Mr Williams realized he was still holding Hilary's duffel coat at arm's length, as though it was something that had once been alive.

'I'll take that,' said James politely, prising the coat from between the headmaster's fingers. Then he stepped outside and closed the door softly behind him.

When James had gone there was an awkward silence. Finally Miss Lewis spoke. 'Did anyone else see that?'

'See what?' said Mrs Murray. '*I* didn't see anything. Did you, Mr Williams?'

'Nothing at all,' said Mr Williams, uncertainly.

The incident was never mentioned again. It was as though the teachers had all had a strange dream that they were embarrassed to talk about. When Miss Lewis and Mrs Murray had left his office, Mr Williams opened his bottom drawer, took a

teaspoon of pink medicine and then got back to work. Miss Lewis returned to class to find James working on a new drawing as though nothing had happened.

When the twins got home Hilary was waiting on the sofa, eating Amanda's chocolate buttons. She jumped up and ran to James and threw her arms around him. 'Thanks, James!' she cried.

James went red and muttered something.

'Thanks for what?' Amanda said, surprised.

'Nothing!' said James.

'It wasn't nothing,' Hilary said 'It was very brave.'

'No it wasn't.'

'Yes it was.' Hilary turned to Amanda. 'He told them I didn't have to go to school because I am an *angel*,' she explained.

There was a short pause. Amanda looked at James, who was busy looking

elsewhere. 'Oh. Did he really?' she said
slowly.

'And I didn't even get to confess,' said
Hilary ruefully. 'Never mind. I'll make it up
to him some other time.'

James looked up, alarmed. 'Oh no!' he
said. 'You don't have to do that.'

But Hilary just smiled. 'Oh yes, I do,'
she said.

12
Icky Vicky

'**V**icky's coming tomorrow,' said
Amanda the following morning.

'Who's Vicky?' asked Hilary.

'She's our cousin,' said James.

Vicky had been to stay with the twins
before. She usually came with her parents,
but this time Auntie Jean and Uncle Bob
had won a holiday for two in Las Vegas, so
Vicky was coming alone. She wasn't

pleased. She said that there was nothing to do at the Mulroneys' house, which wasn't quite fair since the twins always *tried* to include her. But Vicky didn't like indoor games and she didn't like going outside, so it wasn't easy.

'Icky Vicky, we call her,' said James unkindly. 'Whenever she doesn't like something, she *says* she's allergic – but she isn't really. She says she's allergic to *everything*.'

'Everything?'

'Not everything,' said Amanda.

'Nearly everything,' said James.

Hilary looked thoughtful. 'She'll like *me* though,' she said. 'Won't she?'

'Of course she will,' said Amanda.

Vicky arrived the following day with two tight bunches either side of her head and a little pink suitcase. 'What's for dinner?' she demanded, putting down her suitcase and hanging up her coat.

'It's beans on toast,' said Mrs Mulroney. 'You like baked beans, don't you, Vicky?'

Vicky made a face. 'I'm allergic to beans,' she said. 'I only like the juice.'

'I see,' said Mrs Mulroney, perplexed. 'Well, go and say hello to the twins and I'll call you when it's ready,' and she returned to the kitchen to hunt for the sieve.

Vicky found the twins – and Hilary – doing a jigsaw on the floor of their room.

'Hello, Vicky!' said Amanda. 'This is Hilary; she's a friend of ours.'

'Hello,' said Hilary.

'Atchoo!' said Vicky, and she went and sat on the sofa, drumming her heels against the baseboard. She didn't like new people.

'Do you want to do a jigsaw?' asked James.

'I don't like jigsaws,' said Vicky. She carried on kicking her heels, and the others went back to what they had been doing. A little time went by and then Vicky pointed at Hilary and said, 'Why is she wearing that ugly coat?'

The others looked up.

'It's not an ugly coat!' said Amanda
indignantly. (She had gone to school in
that duffel coat for a whole year.)

Vicky did not reply. She got up off
the sofa and went wandering round the
room, picking things up and putting them
down again. 'What's this?' she said
presently.

'It's a feather,' said Amanda. 'It must be
one of Hilary's.'

'She *collects* them?'

'Sort of,' said Amanda.

'Ugh!' said Vicky, flicking it away. 'I'm
allergic to feathers. Get rid of them.'

Hilary got to her feet. 'Perhaps I should
go,' she said.

'No you shouldn't,' said James. 'Sit
down.'

Vicky stamped her foot. 'Get rid of
them,' she demanded. '*All* of them.'

Hilary blanched. 'I can't get rid of

them *all*,' she said.

'Then I will,' said Vicky. 'Where are they?'

'Here,' said Hilary. And before the twins could stop her she got up, threw off her coat and spread her wings. She flapped them a few times for good measure, and sent a flurry of jigsaw pieces across the carpet to settle at Vicky's feet.

'*Hilary*!' cried both the twins.

Vicky's eyes went very wide, and her face paled. Then she took a deep breath and opened her mouth to scream ... but nothing but a high, hoarse whisper came out.

It took a while for the twins to calm Vicky down. Eventually they got her sitting on the sofa with a cold flannel pressed against her forehead. Hilary put her coat back on and was banished to the far side of the room, where she sat mulishly, watching the proceedings. 'It's her own fault,' said

Hilary. 'She asked me where my feathers were.'

'Shut up, Hilary,' said James.

Vicky eyed Hilary from under the flannel. 'Do Auntie Jill and Uncle George know?' she asked.

'No!' said James. 'And you mustn't tell them.'

But Vicky was already struggling to get up.

'We mean it, Vicky,' said James, pushing her back down. 'You're not to tell *anyone* – all right?'

Vicky looked mutinous.

'Promise!'

Vicky pressed her lips together.

'Let her go,' said Hilary from the corner of the room. 'It doesn't matter who she tells. No one will believe her anyway.'

Vicky didn't tell – she just kept dropping hints. After dinner, when Mrs Mulroney got up to clear the plates, Vicky followed her into the kitchen. 'Auntie Jill,' she said. 'Why do you think Hilary wears that coat all the time?'

'I don't know, Vicky,' said Mrs Mulroney, scraping a plate. 'Perhaps she likes it.'

'But what do you think is underneath it, Auntie Jill?'

'I expect Hilary is underneath it,' said Mrs Mulroney, laughing.

Vicky scowled. 'I think she's *weird*,' she said.

When the twins had gone upstairs, Vicky tried Mr Mulroney. 'Look what I found, Uncle George,' she said, twirling a long white feather.

'That's pretty,' said Mr Mulroney.

'Where do you think it's from?'

Mr Mulroney lifted his glasses to take a better look. 'Could it be from a swan, do you think?'

'No,' said Vicky. 'It couldn't. It's not from a bird at all. And guess where I found it?'

'Where?'

'In the twins' bedroom!'

'Oh, well then,' said Mr Mulroney, replacing his glasses, 'it's probably one of theirs. I should put it back where you found it.' And he carried on reading his paper.

Vicky pressed her lips together angrily, and stalked back upstairs. Hilary was nowhere to be seen, but the twins were still doing their jigsaw; it was a picture of lots of coloured kites flying in the sky, and it was nearly finished. Vicky sat on the sofa and watched them for a moment.

'They'll find out sooner or later,' she said.

'Find out what?' said Amanda.

'About the *wings*.'

James sat back on his heels and looked at Vicky. 'And why would that be?'

Vicky shrugged. 'One day,' she said, 'Hilary will *have* to take her coat off.'

'Why?'

'Well – what if someone's hair caught fire,' said Vicky, 'and she had to smother the flames with her duffel coat?'

'Don't be horrible,' said Amanda.

'Or what if she had to catch a baby falling from a skyscraper,' went on Vicky. 'She'd have to take it off then, wouldn't she?'

'What – like Superman?' said James. 'There aren't any skyscrapers round here.'

'All right then – what if someone was being *blown away*,' persisted Vicky, turning a piece of jigsaw over and over in her fingers. 'Like if they were holding on to something *really big* that pulled them into the sky. It *could* happen,' she went on, almost to herself, 'if the person wasn't too heavy, and if their hand was tangled in the string ... Hilary would have to take her coat off then, wouldn't she? To rescue them?'

'Yes, maybe ...' said James impatiently. 'Look! There's one piece missing.'

Vicky smiled to herself and pressed the last corner of the red kite into place.

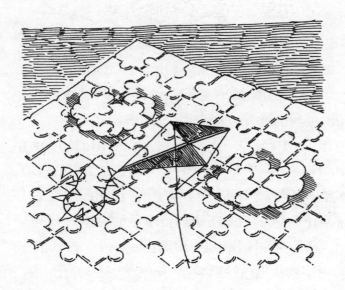

13
The Enormous Kite

'**G**ood grief!' cried Mr Mulroney. 'What on earth is that?'

'It's a kite,' said Vicky.

'But it's enormous!'

'Yep,' said Vicky. She had borrowed an old sheet and the bendy poles from the Mulroneys' tent, and had spent all afternoon cutting and sewing. Now that the kite was spread out on the floor it filled the whole room. There was a long tail of red ribbon, a ball of string to fly it with, and painted right across it was a great big grinning face.

'Can we go and fly it?' asked Vicky.

Mr Mulroney looked doubtful.

'Pleeeease,' said Vicky.

'Well, all right,' said Mr Mulroney. 'If we can get it on the car.'

'Good,' said Vicky. 'Can Hilary come too?'

With help from the whole family, including Hilary, they managed to get the kite on the roof rack and lash it down with ropes. Then they all got in and off they went, with the enormous kite grinning garishly and all the neighbours staring after them.

'This is stupid,' muttered James.

As they picked up speed the kite riffled loudly in the wind like the pages of a book, and by the time they got on the dual carriageway it was so loud that they could barely hear themselves speak.

'DO YOU THINK IT'LL FLY?' shouted
Vicky.

'DEFINITELY,' yelled Hilary.

Vicky smiled and settled back into her
seat.

When they got to the park they
stepped out of the car into bright sunshine
and a gusty wind. Mr and Mrs Mulroney
laid out the picnic blanket and sat down.

'Go and help Vicky fly her kite,' said
Mr Mulroney. 'She's made it especially.'

'If we have to,' grumbled James.

Hilary and Amanda laid the kite on the
grass. They had to kneel on it to keep it
down, for it flapped and snapped in the
breeze like a live thing. Then James and
Vicky unravelled the string to a good
distance.

'What's taking them so long?' said
Hilary. From where they were kneeling it
looked as though Vicky was instructing
James to wind the string around his

wrists …

'I don't know,' said Amanda. 'But I wish they'd hurry up.'

'I'll go and help,' said Hilary. She got up and started towards them – but the moment she stood up the wind caught her side of the kite and lifted it.

'Wait!' cried Amanda, struggling to hold it down. But she was no match for the enormous kite. With a sudden gust it bucked her off and rose straight up into the sky, its painted face leering down in triumph. But that wasn't all. With a yell, James was yanked forward by his wrists. 'Help!' he wailed, staggering after it. But the kite was gathering speed and soon James's feet were barely touching the ground.

'Oh dear,' smirked Vicky.

'Quick!' yelled Amanda.

But before they could catch up with him, James was airborne. 'After him!' cried Mr Mulroney pounding past, followed closely by Mrs Mulroney and Amanda.

Only Vicky and Hilary stayed where they were. Vicky turned to Hilary. 'Well,' she said, 'you'd better *help* him, hadn't you?' She smiled unpleasantly.

Hilary did not reply. She waited until no one was looking, then she slipped off her duffel coat and slung it over one arm, spread her wings and rose gracefully into the air.

The kite was now high above the park. The wind jigged it this way and that, and like a trapeze artist on the end of a rope, James swung from side to side. A faint wail drifted down.

The Mulroneys ran at top speed across the field, past the swings and the picnic area, and everywhere they went people stopped what they were doing and joined in the chase. Eventually there was a long line of people (and dogs, and a lady pushing a joggling baby in a pram) all keen to see where the kite might land. And all the time the grinning kite drifted on above them, with James dangling beneath.

But now the kite was heading towards a spinney of tall elms. For an anxious moment James's foot snagged in the top of the tallest tree – but then the kite tugged him free again and began sinking towards the boating pond on the other side.

'Quick!' cried Mr Mulroney. 'The pond!' He charged straight into the thicket, with the long line of people directly behind him. 'Which way?' he cried.

'This way!' said someone.

'Over here!' yelled someone else.

While they were struggling through the undergrowth, Hilary (noticed by no one) sailed gracefully over the treetops. If anyone had been on the other side they might have seen the kite deposit James smack into the middle of the boating pond, and witnessed his feeble splashing. Then they might have seen Hilary swoop down

like an angel out of the sky, seize him by the collar and drag him to the edge of the pond. But nobody did – they were all too busy trying to find their way through the trees. By the time they emerged it was all over. The kite was undulating on the water like a great big grinning jellyfish, and James was sitting on the shore coughing and spluttering. Hilary was standing nearby, doing up the buttons on her duffel coat.

'James!' cried Mrs Mulroney, rushing forward and wrapping her cardigan around him. 'Are you all right? What happened?'

But before he could reply, Vicky had pushed to the front of the crowd. 'I know!' she yelled. 'I know what happened!'

'You do?' said Mr Mulroney.

'Yes!' Vicky pointed at Hilary. 'It's her! She … she …'

'She what?'

Vicky shifted uncomfortably.

'She … she …'

Everyone stared at her.

'She, um ...'

Then suddenly, in front of all those people, Vicky's nerve failed. She looked at the ground. 'She pulled him out,' she said softly.

'*Hooray!*' cried the crowd, and they hoisted Hilary onto their shoulders and carried her back through the trees, singing.

Vicky trailed behind them, sulking and whacking at flowers with a stick.

When they got back to the car James was wrapped in the picnic blanket and given hot tea from the thermos while Mrs Mulroney rubbed his back vigorously to get his circulation going.

'He'll survive,' said Mr Mulroney.

'Yes – thanks to Hilary!' said Mrs Mulroney. She laughed. 'You've got a guardian angel, James!' she teased. 'We'll be forever grateful, won't we?'

'Yes,' mumbled James.

'What do you say, James?' prompted Mr Mulroney.

'Thank you, Hilary.'

'That's all right,' said Hilary. She settled back with a smug expression and hummed softly to herself all the way home. Vicky, on the other hand, sat in the opposite corner with her arms folded and didn't say another word to Hilary or to the twins for the rest of her stay. And she didn't say much to Mr and Mrs Mulroney, either.

14
Hilary Goes Home

After Vicky left there came one of those heavy grey days with an iron gust to the air like when it's going to snow. Christmas was only a week away, and the twins were busy wrapping presents and signing name tags.

'I'm glad Vicky's gone,' said James. 'I like it best when we're on our own.'

'Yes,' said Amanda. 'I don't *mind*

having visitors, but sometimes they stay too long.'

'Much too long,' agreed James.

Hilary was thoughtful. 'How long is too long?' she asked.

'Depends on the person,' said James.

'Have *I* stayed too long?'

'Of course not!' cried Amanda. 'What makes you think that?'

'Oh! Nothing,' said Hilary.

The twins returned to their wrapping, but Hilary sat twiddling a piece of ribbon, thinking far-away thoughts.

'I suppose it's time I was getting back,' she said presently.

'Back *home*?' said Amanda.

'Yes.'

'But I thought you were staying with *us* for Christmas,' said Amanda, crestfallen.

'Nah,' said Hilary. She twisted the bit of ribbon around her finger. 'I have to open all my presents.'

James and Amanda exchanged a

glance. 'You have Christmas too?' said James.

'Of course!' said Hilary. But she didn't look at them. 'I get so many presents it sometimes takes me a week to unwrap them all!'

'But I thought—'

'Yep,' Hilary went on. 'Christmas is *huge* back home. All the games – and the stories. Wow!' She rolled her eyes.

'Well,' said James, 'I suppose you'll be glad to get back, then.'

'Yep.'

But Hilary seemed a little melancholy and didn't say much for the rest of the evening. And later, when the twins went downstairs to decorate the tree, Hilary climbed out onto the roof and sat beside the chimney, hugging her knees and gazing at the stars.

'Aren't you coming in?' asked James, when they came to bed.

'Not yet,' said Hilary.

James left the skylight open for her. 'Hilary's very quiet,' he remarked, switching off the bedside light.

'Yes,' said Amanda. 'I thought she was staying with us for Christmas. She never mentioned going home before.'

'No,' said James.

There was silence while they both lay in the dark, thinking.

'I think she made it up,' said Amanda, eventually.

'Made what up?'

'About the presents. I bet they don't even *have* presents where she comes from.'

'Why would she say they do, then?'

'She doesn't want us to feel sorry for her.'

'Well, that's silly,' said James. 'Why doesn't she just stay with us?'

'Maybe she thinks she's outstayed her welcome.'

James was quiet for a moment. 'Well,

we'll tell her we *want* her to stay,' he said firmly, 'when she comes back in.'

'All right,' said Amanda.

But before long the twins were sound asleep, their double breaths rising and falling in the darkness. And while they slept, Hilary slipped back through the skylight and closed it very gently so as not to wake them. But she didn't go to bed – she took off her duffel coat and folded it carefully, then took off her sandals and socks and arranged them beside the sofa. Then she tiptoed across the room and crept softly down the stairs.

The house was quiet. Downstairs the hall clock was tocking peacefully, and the heating gurgled somewhere far away. Hilary tiptoed into the front room and stopped short, clapping a hand to her mouth … For there, standing in the bay window, was the Christmas tree. The fairy lights cast a speckled pattern round the walls. Little red apples and silver stars and papier-mâché bells hung from the tips of the branches – and there were things the twins had made at school: painted pine cones and paper snowflakes. Hilary crept up to the tree and touched a tiny gold parcel wrapped with a bow. It swung gently.

Hilary turned her attention to the heap of presents beneath the tree ... big ones, small ones, all in different patterned paper. She squatted to read the name tags, but the scribbles all looked the same to her. Then she noticed that one of the tags had a picture on it instead of writing: a picture of a stick figure with a triangle for a dress and two big wings. Hilary gave a muffled cry of astonishment – here was a present especially for her!

Hilary had never opened a present before. As quickly as she could she ripped off the paper and found inside a pair of thick red socks and matching mittens and a long red scarf with tassels on the end. She

put them all on and stepped back to take one last look at the tree – and that was when she saw it.

At the tip top of the tree was a small doll in a white dress. It had bare feet and windswept hair, and a pair of feathered wings spread out behind. Hilary clapped her mittens in delight, and the tree lights blurred through her tears. For there, in pride of place at the top of the Christmas tree, was *Hilary herself*! Hilary smiled. Now she knew that they wouldn't forget her.

When the twins awoke it was morning, and their mother was calling.

'Eight o'clock! Breakfast!'

The twins were awake straight away, as you are when the first thing you remember is that it's a holiday and it's nearly Christmas. They were already dressed and heading for the stairs before they realized that Hilary had gone. Amanda's old brown duffel coat lay folded neatly on the sofa;

the sandals sat together on the floor.

'Maybe she's on the roof,' said James. He opened the skylight – but there was nobody out there. 'Hilary?' he cried, flinging open the wardrobe. But inside there was nothing but clothes hanging silently, and a few squashed shoes – and under the beds he found nothing but dust and a couple of feathers. 'She can't have just *gone*,' he cried.

But it appeared that she had. A heavy silence seemed to fill the whole house; it felt very empty without her.

'I expect there's a big demand for guardian angels,' said Amanda soberly. 'Especially at this time of year.'

'But we never even said goodbye!'

'No.'

'Wait a minute!' James had noticed something. He rushed to the sofa and pulled a piece of paper out from under the pillow. 'What's this?'

'A note! What's it say?'

'Nothing,' said James, disappointed. 'It's only pictures.'

But Amanda took it from him. 'It *does* say something,' she said. 'Look!'

And so it did.

It can get cold flying at night, even when you're wearing woolly red socks and mittens. And tonight is a crisp, clear night and the rooftops are silvered with frost. There goes Hilary now! Off she flies, full of the cheerful satisfaction of the accomplished do-gooder – skimming across the tiles with her red socks kicking and her red scarf streaming out behind her like a banner. Oops! She nearly snagged her scarf on that chimney pot. 'Careful, Hilary! Chimneys can be dangerous!' But I'm not sure she can hear us now – she's too far off.
'Bye, Hilary! Until next time!'

Hilary's note says
'I will be back'

Praise for

THE FISH IN ROOM 11
by Heather Dyer

This is a quirky, charming book, funny and imaginative.
OBSERVER

. . . refreshing and breezy, rather like the sea air.
SUNDAY TIMES

A breath of fresh, sea air.
SCOTSMAN

. . . as clear and sparkling as the sea in the summer sun . . .
this has all the joyous playfulness of a little classic.
TIMES

. . . a zany, delightful story . . .
INDEPENDENT

The Fish in Room 11 *has all the ingredients of a*
classic children's novel . . .
IRISH TIMES

Its gorgeous, timeless story is the reading equivalent of a
favourite cosy blanket: warm and reassuring.
BBC PARENTING

A very funny story . . . it is a real novel for young
readers in the style of Roald Dahl.
CAROUSEL

Readers who love Roald Dahl's James and the
Giant Peach *will adore this funny, old-fashioned*
orphan-finds-a-new-family tale.
BOOKLIST